# BIBI TAKES FLIGHT

# MICHEL GAY

# BIBI TAKES FLIGHT

Morrow Junior Books / New York

Library of Congress Cataloging-in-Publication Data
Gay, Michel.
Bibi takes flight.
Translation of: Biboundé.
Summary: A young penguin resolves to learn how to
fly rather than swim in the cold ocean.
[1. Penguins—Fiction.   2. Flight—Fiction]
I. Title
PZ7.G238Bh   1988       [E]        87-28262
ISBN 0-688-06828-6
ISBN 0-688-06829-4 (lib. bdg.)

# BIBI TAKES FLIGHT

Bibi and his father, the penguin king, were playing in the snow.

"Ready?" the king asked.

"Ready," said Bibi. "I want to go really high. I want to fly!"

The king laughed. He tossed Bibi high into the air—*one, two, three* times. "Penguins can't fly, little Bibi," he said. "I thought you knew."

It was getting late. The king was out of breath. It was time to go home for breakfast with the queen.

The queen made wonderful chocolate pancakes. Bibi ate six. "Why can't penguins fly?" he asked.

"We just can't," his father told him. "Now finish your breakfast, Bibi. All my subjects are here for inspection."

The penguins stood in a straight line. The king inspected them from head to toe. He was proud of their shining coats and spotless feet.

Bibi just hid because he knew what was coming next.

The minute inspection was over the penguins dived into the sea. They laughed and splashed in the foaming water. The sea looked very, very cold to Bibi—much too cold for a little penguin.

So Bibi stayed on shore. He loved to watch the birds as they soared in the sky. One was coming toward him now, closer and closer . . .

And then *whoosh*—the queen was skimming across the snow, straight for Bibi.

*Ouf!* She reached him just in time.

"Keep away from my son, you bully," she shouted. The bird flew away, its feathers drooping.

"Not all birds are friendly," the queen warned Bibi. "Some eat little penguins! If you don't want to play in the water, then you will have to stay with me."

Poor Bibi. Now he had nothing to do but push his mother's ball of yarn back and forth and listen to a lot of boring conversation. This wasn't how he had planned to spend his morning at all!

The wind was gusting, harder and harder. "My yarn!" cried the queen, chasing after the runaway blue ball.

But when she looked up, there was Bibi. "'Bye, Mommy," Bibi called, waving as he sailed by. "I'm flying."

Bibi heard his mother shouting "Come back! Come back!"
But the wind carried him on.

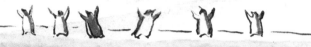

Below him was the coldest looking water he had ever seen.
Bibi wanted to go back to his mother, but he knew he couldn't.
I'm not really flying, he told himself. I'm only floating on the
wind. Bibi was very disappointed.

In a little while the wind set him gently down on an iceberg.

Bibi looked around. In the distance he spied a young walrus and a puffin.

Bibi was glad to have some company. "Hellooo," he called. "Wait for me!"

But they didn't.

That's strange, Bibi thought. What could have made them run away? Then he understood. High in the sky, getting closer and closer, was a big bird! Bibi waved his flippers, hoping for another gust of wind to take him far away. But none came.

Then Bibi made himself very small, hoping the bird wouldn't spot him. He remained still for a long time.

Finally, Bibi looked up. There hadn't been a bird after all. Bibi had seen airplanes before, but never so close. He crept closer for a better look.

The pilot was climbing out of the cockpit.
He was carrying some kind of tool.

The pilot slipped and the tool went flying. "Oh no," he cried, "my wrench!"

Slowly, the wrench sank down into the icy water. "I must have that wrench," the pilot said. He looked at Bibi. Bibi looked at the water below. He knew that humans could not swim where it was so cold. But a penguin could.

Bibi plunged in.

What a surprise! Bibi thought, This water isn't cold at all—as a matter of fact, I like it!

Bibi gave the pilot his wrench. "Thank you," the pilot said. "My name is Frank. How can I thank you enough?"

Bibi didn't want thanks. He wanted to help repair the plane. He and Frank worked hard. Bibi talked nonstop about how he came to be on the iceberg. "Of course," he said, "I know I wasn't really flying."

Frank tried the engine. It worked!

"Shall I take you home?" he asked Bibi.
"Oh, yes," Bibi answered happily. "Now I will truly fly."

Off they flew, over the clear blue water, the crisp white snow, and the shining ice—and right through a flock of tough-looking birds.

"They won't bother you anymore," Frank told Bibi, "now that they see how you can fly."

All too soon, Bibi was home. Slowly he got down from the plane. "Don't worry," Frank said, wrapping his scarf around the little penguin prince. "We'll meet again."

Then he flew away.

The king was so happy to see Bibi that he hugged him tight and threw him into the air. Soon Bibi was being tossed from penguin to penguin like a rubber ball.

"How many times do you want our son to be carried off by the wind?" said the queen, scolding her husband. "Bibi is staying right here with me!"

What can I do? Bibi wondered. But then he had an idea.

"Let's have an inspection," he said loudly to the king, "to celebrate my return!"

The penguins stood in a straight line. The king inspected them from head to toe.

Bibi stood proudly, even with grease from the airplane all over his chest. "Don't worry," he said to the penguin next to him, "it will wash off when we swim."

When the inspection was over, Bibi dived straight into the water. The king and queen could hardly believe their eyes! The king jumped into the water, too, and he swam majestically beside his son.

The queen and her friends brought a picnic to the sea.
"Here's to our brave Prince Bibi," the penguins cried, "the
very first penguin to fly!"
Bibi just smiled and kept on paddling.